A VERY BRAVE Witch

Alison McGHEE

Harry BLISS

A PAULA WISEMAN BOOK
Simon & Schuster Books for Young Readers
New York London Toronto Sydney

SIMON & SCHUSTER BOOKS FOR YOUNG READERS

An imprint of Simon & Schuster Children's Publishing Division

1230 Avenue of the Americas, New York, New York 10020

For information about special discounts for bulk purchases, please contact

Simon & Schuster Special Sales at 1-866-506-1949 or business@simonandschuster.com.

The Simon & Schuster Speakers Bureau can bring authors to your live event.

For more information or to book an event, contact the Simon & Schuster Speakers Bureau at

1-866-248-3049 or visit our website at www.simonspeakers.com.

Also available in a Simon & Schuster Books for Young Readers hardcover edition

Book design by Einav Aviram

Hand lettering by Paul Colin

The illustrations for this book are rendered in black ink and watercolor

on Arches 90 lb. watercolor paper.

Manufactured in China

0412 SCP

First Simon & Schuster Books for Young Readers paperback edition August 2011

4 6 8 10 9 7 5

The Library of Congress has cataloged a previous edition as follows:

McGhee, Alison, 1960-

A very brave witch / Alison McGhee ; illustrated by Harry Bliss. — 1st ed.

p. cm.

"A Paula Wiseman book."

Summary: A young witch describes what she does on Halloween, her favorite holiday.

ISBN 978-0-689-86730-9 (hc)

[1. Halloween—Fiction. 2. Witches—Fiction.] I. Bliss, Harry, 1964- ill. II. Title.

PZ7.M4784675Ve 2006 [E]—dc22 2005016108

ISBN 978-1-4169-8670-6 (unjacketed edition)

ISBN 978-0-689-86731-6 (pbk)

To Holly McGhee—A. M.

For Charley and Ben Bliss—H. B.